There was a time when man was especially aware of the world around him and spoke a silent language with the living things that make up our planet. This was a silent language of love and respect and it made all living things equal in the story of Life.

Some of the people who could do this were called Saints, a title that means they shared a deep love for God and for the Beauty of the Universe and found in their animal friends companionship, understanding and love.

This silent language is not a secret one - nor do only saints know how to speak it. Silent means inside ourselves, within our thoughts and emotions, and because everyone has an inside and has thoughts and emotions, we all can speak it. All we have to do is listen and learn from our animal friends and the growing things around us.

—A.M.G.

SPECIAL FRIENDS:
TALES OF SAINTS AND ANIMALS

ARLENE MARGUERITE GRASTON

A Bantam Skylark Book®
Toronto • New York • London • Sydney

With love
I dedicate this book to:
Jeremy, Michael,
Rachel, Amber,
Baby, and Mimi

RL 5,   010 and up

SPECIAL FRIENDS: TALES OF SAINTS AND ANIMALS
A Bantam Skylark Book / November 1981

ISBN 0-553-15084-7

Published simultaneously in the United States and Canada

Bantam Books are published by Bantam Books, Inc. Its trade-
mark, consisting of the words "Bantam Books" and the por-
trayal of a rooster, is Registered in U.S. Patent and Trademark
Office and in other countries. Marca Registrada. Bantam
Books, Inc., 666 Fifth Avenue, New York, New York 10103.

PRINTED IN THE UNITED STATES OF AMERICA

0 9 8 7 6 5 4 3 2 1

Off the coast of Ireland, centuries ago, there lived a priest named Ciaran who wanted to become a hermit in order to lead a more holy life.

Ciaran decided to live on a quiet wooded island and on this island he built a little house and then he began to build a rustic chapel.

And so began his life of solitude, but it didn't last long, because the other inhabitants of the island had something else in mind. Every time Ciaran was deep in study or lost in meditation - the chirping of the birds and the chatter of the chipmunks and the flutter of the butterflies would interrupt his thoughts and would call his attention to the life around him. He soon learned to love the busy activity in the woods and allowed the animals and the flowers and the trees to teach him all the wonderful things they knew.

It wasn't long before two very special
friends came to help him build his little
church...a tall and graceful deer and her
baby fawn.

They were shy at first but Ciaran had a gentle manner that made them feel so welcome that they decided to stay. Soon they were busily hauling logs and pulling stones, and before they knew it, the little church was built.

The two little deer became the first parish-ioners to attend mass and hear the sermon in St. Ciaran's chapel.

One day a wild boar happened to be walking by St. Ciaran's house where he and the deer were hard at work.

Now, deer and wild boar are mortal enimies and when they meet terrible, terrible things can happen!

At first everyone held his breath...but once the first shock was over it became clear that nothing terrible was going to happen. Ciaran was a man of love and had learned a special silent way of building trust and friendship with the animals and greeted the new arrival as if he was a long lost friend. The deer joined in, and a new member was added to the family.

Soon after that a handsome grey wolf joined the growing group. And he proved to be a brave and strong addition and happily returned the love that he was given.

One night while he was out looking for his food, a particularly lazy badger wandered into Ciaran's little camp. He liked what he saw so much that he decided to move in, even though he planned to sleep the whole day through just as he had always done.

But Ciaran had other thoughts about this and told him, "You are welcome to join us. But you, too, must have a special task for there is so much to do to make our household work. Would you bring sticks back for us each night, for our fire?"

The little badger thought about that awhile (for he was *very* lazy) and finally agreed. And he was very happy that he did for he was an important part of a loving family.

As the days drifted busily by Ciaran began to notice that two curious eyes had been peering at him and his little family from behind the trees. Once, he even caught a glimpse of a bushy red tail and two pointed ears.

It seemed that a cautious little fox was viewing the goings on, not quite certain what to make of everything.

Foxes just don't come right up and say hello for they are sly and cunning and like to think things over. So Ciaran patiently waited for the animal to become brave.

One day the little fox crept carefully from behind a big tree and slowly wagged his tail at Ciaran.

"Welcome little friend," said Ciaran, "don't be afraid for we have only peace and love for you and if you will learn to trust us you will find a happy home here. And we will be happy you came."

With that the little fox wagged his tail very hard and even smiled with his eyes. And that was how the last member of the family was added.

They lived together happily, this little forest family, and the woods are still remembering their story.

Once there lived, long, long ago an Irish monk named Coleman. He was a simple man who lived for goodness and who gave up the world of people to lead a life of prayer.

He did however, choose three unusual animal friends who brought him many pleasures.

There was a dashing rooster...

a lively little mouse...

and . . . a tiny, tiny fly!

Now, Coleman was very smart but he did often have his head up in the clouds and he very much needed his three little friends to get him through the day.

Early each morning when the sun began to shine, the dashing rooster would start his crowing and wake Coleman, who was known for sleeping very soundly. Thanks to him, Coleman was never late to mass.

And there were times at prayers and study when Coleman was known to fall asleep or daydream. That was when the faithful little mouse would step out from under his robe and nibble energetically on his toes to wake him up...and bring his attention back to his work.

And when his attention had been returned
to his work...he found that the tiny, tiny
fly (who had been keeping a close watch on
things) had kept his book open to the right
page.

As happens in life, Coleman's little friends died one by one - but still his heart was full with memory. And he said to all who would listen that a man was rich forever if he had the faithful love of a friend...and he, Coleman, had had *three* faithful friends.

In the countryside of France, a long time ago, lived a little shepherdess named Germaine. Although she was a plain child, she was sweet and gentle. And although she was loving she had never known love and kindness, for her mother had died when she was very little and her father was very mean to her.

She was made to do all the family chores from sweeping the barn to washing the dishes and was given only the table scraps for her supper.

She was not even allowed to live in the
house with the rest of the family but was
sent each night, by her step-mother to sleep
in the barn where the hay was her bed.

Still, Germaine found happiness as she
faithfully filled her thoughts with God and
learned to turn all bad things into good.

Each day she gave a heartful of thanks
for having the comfort of her good friends
the sheep, who would spend hours and hours
quietly listening as she told them marvelous
stories about the wonders of God's world.

Early every morning Germaine would make her way to the village church to attend mass.

One day, without warning, her father was waiting there for her. He was very, very angry.

"You are a terrible child," he shouted. "I forbid you to go to mass and leave your sheep unattended. Go back to the pasture at once!"

Germaine dutifully did as she was told but her heart was heavy and sad. She wanted so much to attend mass but did not want to disobey her father or leave her sheep unattended.

So she turned to God once more in prayer and asked what she might do.

God and all the creatures in His Heaven must have heard her simple plea for every morning a Shepherd Angel came to guard Germaine's sheep so she could go to mass.

M any, many years ago, in the fifth century, there lived a remarkable old monk named St. Jerome.

His greatest pleasure was to study and learn and he spent most of his day with his nose buried in mountains of books and manuscripts.

Because he was a man of prayer and because he had devoted his life to the word of God, he was given the special task of translating the Bible from the ancient languages into Latin - which is what people spoke in his day.

His work kept him very busy and he had no time to spend with people. This was all right, for he was a bit unsociable and much preferred the company of his books.

In order to go about his work without interruption, he went to live in a desert near the town of Bethlehem, where Jesus was born.

Hidden in a little monastery under the hot desert sun he and his fellow monks settled down to long quiet days of thoughtful study.

One peaceful evening as the sun was beginning to set a very unusual thing happened...something big and furry slowly made its way up the monastery path!

It couldn't be...but it was...

a LION!

A huge, ferocious lion was coming up the monastery path!

How terrible! Never having seen a wild beast before the monks dropped their books, their brooms and their water buckets to run for safety.

But not Jerome. Wise man that he was,
he quickly saw that the lion was limping
and that something was in his paw causing
the poor animal much pain.

"You are welcome here, oh noble friend
of the wild," said Jerome, taking the big
throbbing paw into his own gentle hand.

"We have a humble home, but it will
honor us to care for your wound and to
make you comfortable and well again."

And so, cautiously, the lion was brought into the monastery. And while the monks watched from a safe distance, Jerome tenderly removed a tremendous splinter and cleaned the wound and made a very big bandage for a very big paw.

The monks, who had great faith in St. Jerome, now saw that there was nothing to fear from this big and unexpected guest who seemed to be as shy as they were. They came forward to meet the beautiful animal and all became good friends.

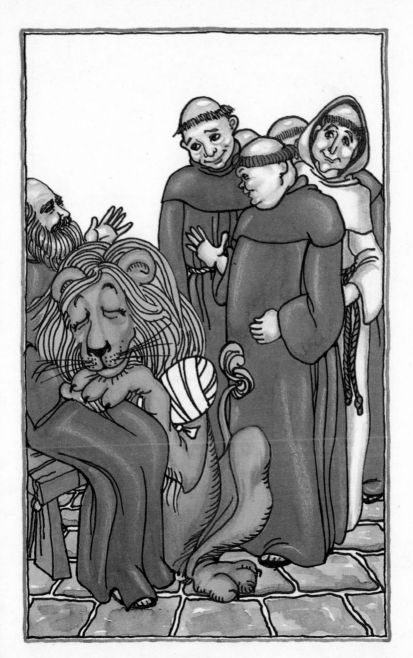

Peace and quiet soon returned to the monastery and the days went by, each gently slipping one into the other. Everyone had a special and important task designed to keep the little community happily rolling along.

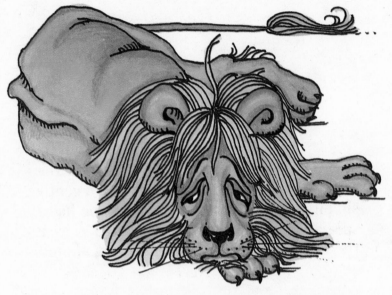

Everyone had something to contribute, everyone, that is, except the lion. By this time he was well again and spent his days lying around moping...and moping...and moping.

"Well this just won't do!" said Jerome to the other monks. "We must think about what special work our friend could do to make him feel important and let him know that he is needed."

So they put their heads together and thought.

"I know!" said one of the monks, "our good friend the donkey goes out each day to fetch us stones for building and wood for making fire. It is such hard and lonely work that he needs a good and faithful companion to help with his heavy chore."

And so it was that each new day found this curious twosome going out, side by side, into the wilderness to bring back the much needed stones and firewood for a grateful and busy little community...where everyone had a special and important job to do.

In Lima, Peru lived a man named St. Martin de Porres. He was known all over the land as a man of great kindness who spent his life helping the poor.

He lived in a monastery where he and the other monks devoted their time to acts of charity. It was Martin's special job to feed the needy and hungry.

They came in long lines bringing their empty stomachs and broken hearts. And Martin never tired of giving to each a warm bowl of food for their bodies and loving, kind words for their souls.

It wasn't long before the stray dogs and cats of Lima heard about this wonderful man, and soon they too, formed long lines waiting for the food and gentle words that Martin gave so generously.

Even the monastery mice had their special place in Martin's heart. He would leave little trails of bread crumbs all over the monastery grounds so that his little friends would not have to go searching for food.

No one was forgotten in Martin's world.

There lived in Italy, many many years ago, the most gentle of all the people who loved God. He was a monk whose heart was like a child's - for he viewed the world with constant wonderment. His name was St. Francis of Assisi.

He was a friend to all living things. He called the Earth his Sister and delighted in all the remarkable things that grew out of her Nature...the Animals, the Flowers, the Trees, the Rain, and the Thunder.

His brothers, the Fish, were his eager listeners and would stand, fascinated, in neat little rows while he told them wonderful stories about the Universe.

And his Sister Birds would come from far away places to share with Francis the wonders they had seen.

He loved the Sun, and the Moon, and all the Stars and the Planets in our Sky.

He loved Everything and told anyone who
would listen of the joy he felt at being alive.

One day, in the middle of summer when the sun was high in the sky, Francis arrived at the usually peaceful little village of Gubbio.

But this day there was great turmoil in the streets and the people were running into their houses in fear.

"Help us Francis," they cried when they saw him. "There is a wild wolf loose in the hills and he is attacking our people and animals! We must protect our town from this dangerous beast."

Francis believed that all living things were children of God and that the wolf was probably hungry and frightened. So with a confident and brave heart, Francis went looking for him to bring help and friendship.

The beast was snarling as the gentle monk approached and seemed about to jump ferociously on Francis when suddenly... he stopped.

With puzzlement in his eyes he watched as Francis slowly held out his arms and said, "Brother Wolf, in the name of all that is peaceful and loving, put aside your anger and your fear. You and I are created to be friends and companions along the path of life. The villagers are your friends and wish you well. Stop your killing and be at peace. You will never have to go hungry again."

And incredibly, the frightened beast was soothed, relieved to be free of his fury. He bowed his head and gently placed his paw in Francis' outstretched hands.

The wolf never again caused the villagers to fear him. He became a familiar sight as he freely roamed the happy and safe streets of the little town of Gubbio.

ABOUT THE AUTHOR

ARLENE MARGUERITE GRASTON grew up in France and came to New York when she was 22. Although it took a little getting used to, she now loves New York and can't imagine living anywhere else. She has a studio called Visibles and she designs gold and diamond jewelry, posters and costumes for the theater, and designs and writes copy for magazines and advertising agencies.